HOGWASH!

by
Karma Wilson

illustrated by
Jim McMullan

LB
Little, Brown and Company
New York Boston

One warm day in early May,
Farmer had a plan
To spring-clean all his animals
Till each was spic 'n' span.

Farmer fetched a pail and soap,
Put on his cleaning duds,
Then went out to the waterspout
And lathered up some suds.

He washed the horses, ducks and cows,
The goats, the cats and dogs.
Everything went dandy...
Until Farmer reached his hogs.

The pigs got out their toolbox,
And they boarded up their pen.
No matter WHAT poor Farmer said,
They wouldn't let him in!

NO HOGWASH
FOR US TODAY.
PIGS LOVE DIRT—
SO GO AWAY!

Farmer scratched his head and thought,
Then said, “Here’s what I’ll do.
Since those pigs have locked me out,
I’ll spray some water through!”

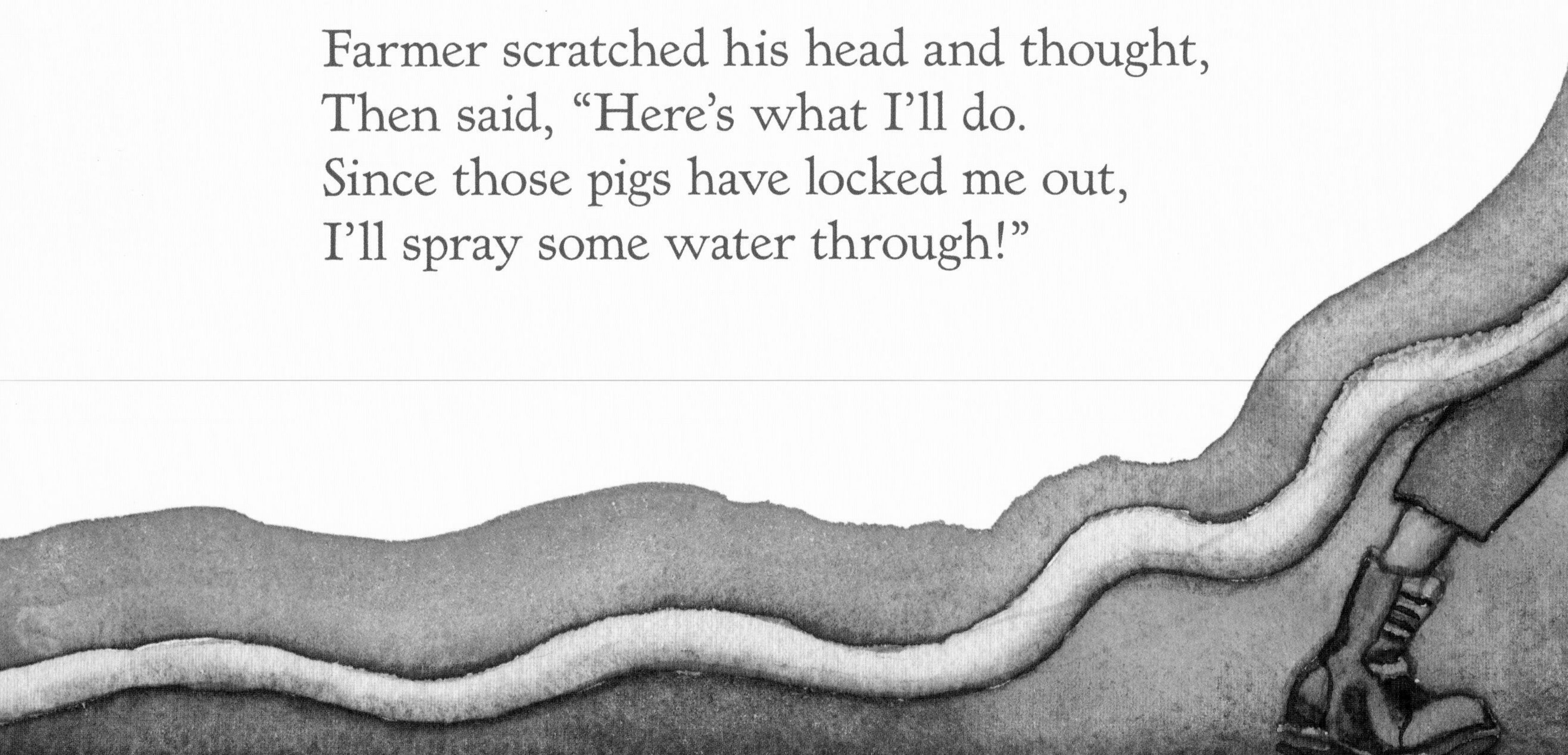

He dragged a hose up to the fence
And turned it on full power.
"If you pigs won't take a bath,
I'll give you all a shower!"

The pigs got their umbrellas out
And put on rubber suits.
They stomped through muddy puddles
In their shiny yellow boots.

They all dug in and made mud pies.
They had a mud-ball war!
They splished and splashed
and hammed it up,
More filthy than before.

Farmer stomped his feet and yelled,
"You oinkers got me riled!"
They still refused to take a bath.
Those pigs had gone hog wild!

KEEP YOUR SOAP
AND BUCKET, BUD.
THANKS FOR
MAKING ALL
THIS MUD!

"Suey, suey!" Farmer called.
"I've got some mash and oats."
The pigs were not impressed at all.
Go feed it to the goats!

Farmer lied, "It's the pizza man.
I've got your pizza pie."
The pigs weren't fooled one little bit.
Just leave it by the sty.

Farmer muttered,
stomped and growled,
"You're stubborn
and pigheaded!"
The pigs just snorted
with disgust.
No hogwash—
just forget it!

No matter what the farmer tried,
They wouldn't let him come inside.
Farmer pondered for a while,
Farmer grinned a crafty smile.

Farmer yelled,
"That's it, by gosh!"
Look out, hogs...

It's
time...
to
WASH!

"I've finally found the perfect plan.
I know just what to do!"
Then Farmer filled his crop dust plane
With water and shampoo.

He climbed into the pilot's seat
And set off on his mission.
He flew above the pigpen
Armed with sudsy ammunition.

Farmer cried, "It's washing day!
Look out, piggies! Bombs away!"

Farmer swooped to make a pass.
Farmer's plane ran out of gas.
Farmer gulped. The engine sputtered.
"Just my luck," the farmer muttered.

Down the plane went, like a rock.
"Look out, I'm gonna CRASH!"
The pigs began to squeal in fright....
Clunk! Clank! Bang! Boom! Bash!

CLUNK!
CLANK!
BOOM!
BANG!

All the horses, ducks and cows,
The goats, the cats and dogs
Ran to help the farmer,
And they found him with those hogs.

There was Farmer, soaked in grime,
having quite a splendid time!

He joined the pigs and made mud pies.
He wallowed all around.
He splished and splashed and hammed it up
And rolled upon the ground.

Farmer saw the animals
And called out, "Come and play!
The mud is great, let's celebrate.
We'll bathe some other day."

From then on Farmer never tried
To wash his hogs again.
But every other day he took
A mud bath in their pen.

To Debi Brannan, congratulations on all you've accomplished.
You're amazing, and that's no hogwash.
—K.W.

For Kate
—J.M.

 Little, Brown and Company • Hachette Book Group • 237 Park Avenue, New York, NY 10017 • Visit our website at www.lb-kids.com • Little, Brown and Company is a division of Hachette Book Group, Inc.

Library of Congress Cataloging-in-Publication Data

Wilson, Karma.
Hogwash / by Karma Wilson ; illustrated by Jim McMullan. — 1st ed.
p. cm.
Summary: When his stubborn pigs refuse a sudsy cleaning, a determined farmer learns that mud baths can be just as fun.
ISBN 978-0-316-98840-7
[1. Stories in rhyme. 2. Pigs—Fiction. 3. Farmers—Fiction. 4. Cleanliness—Fiction. 5. Baths—Fiction.] I. McMullan, Jim, 1936- ill. II. Title.
PZ8.3.W6976Hm 2011
[E]—dc22
2010019754

First Edition: June 2011 • ISBN 978-0-316-98840-7 • 10 9 8 7 6 5 4 3 2 • SC • Printed in China
The illustrations for this book were done in watercolor. The text was set in Hadriano Light.
Book design by Patti Ann Harris.